On a Cold Christmas Night

Lyman Hafen

Covenant Communications, Inc.

God's gifts, unlike seasonal gifts, are eternal and unperishable, constituting a continuing Christmas which is never over!

—Elder Neal A. Maxwell
(*The Christmas Scene,* Bookcraft, 1994, 4-5.)

Cover images © Photodisc Green

Cover design copyrighted 2003 by Covenant Communications, Inc.

Published by Covenant Communications, Inc.
American Fork, Utah

Copyright © 2003 by Lyman Hafen

All rights reserved. No part of this book may be reproduced in any format or in any medium without the written permission of the publisher, Covenant Communications, Inc., P.O. Box 416, American Fork, UT 84003. The views expressed herein are the responsibility of the author and do not necessarily represent the position of Covenant Communications, Inc.

This is a work of fiction. The characters, names, incidents, places, and dialogue are products of the author's imagination, and are not to be construed as real.

Printed in Canada
First Printing: December 2003

08 07 06 05 04 03 02 01   10 9 8 7 6 5 4 3 2 1

ISBN 1-59156-306-2

Christmas Day was drawing heavily to a close. The bright light of morning had crossed over to the gray shadows of evening. Where there had been joy and laughter there was now complacency and silence. Where there had been energy and goodwill, now there was weariness and indifference. The day was ending like any other built up to be more than it can ever be.

Yet it had been a perfect Christmas morning. My seven-year-old daughter had awakened my wife and me well before daylight. Our Sara, a radiant, blue-eyed girl with curly brown hair, had been looking forward to Christmas with the full intensity of her heart for weeks. I felt that precious little heart beating like the breast of a captured bird as she snuggled in bed between us and began to make her case that it was time to get up.

"It's too early," I whispered. "Santa probably hasn't even been here yet."

"Oh yes! He's been here, Daddy," Sara said. "I already looked."

"That's against the rules," I said.

"I know," Sara said. "But I couldn't help it. It's taken so long for Christmas to come. We've got to get up and open the presents."

And so we did. Sara awoke her little brother Jake, and my wife and I followed them down the hallway and into the living room that was awash with the red, blue, and green lights of the Christmas tree. For two hours there was magic in that room. There was exultant laughter and blissful smiles; there was so much pent-up joy in the house I thought it might at any moment explode.

Now it was all a hollow echo. Our stomachs were full of turkey and rich pie, and the living room was strewn with piles of expensive gifts, but the day's early promise had vanished as completely as the brightly wrapped packages that had sat for weeks beneath the tree. Through the long holiday season it had all built to a high Christmas-morning crescendo, but now whatever it was we had been anticipating had come and gone, and we were left in its wake with wanting hearts and sagging spirits. Something very important was missing.

I lay fully extended in my recliner, looking up through the celestial window in our living room. Out in the gray twilight of dusk, I saw the first star of evening appear. As I struggled for an answer to what it was that was missing, I felt a gentle tap on my shoulder. It was Sara.

"Daddy?" she said.

I snapped out of my trance and turned my head toward her. She was so close that the tip of my nose nearly brushed the tip of hers. The brilliant light of the morning had gone out of her eyes, but they still managed to hold all the hope of the world. And in those longing eyes, in that revealing moment, I saw all eternity.

"I wish Christmas wouldn't be over," she said.

I sat up in the chair and lifted my forlorn little daughter onto my lap. She curled into a ball in my arms and snuggled her head beneath my chin. I held her tight and felt as if I could hold her safely away from the cold world out there, away from the distress, the disappointment, the disillusionment of this life. In that quiet moment I realized that I could also be shielded from those very things. My Father could protect my heart from that emptiness even better than my arms could keep it from touching Sara. The quiet whisper of the Spirit overwhelmed me. My heart had never burned so bright with love, nor had it ever been so charged with a desire for that love to fill the heart of another. I looked out the window again at the single shining star in the heavens. I wanted to believe that what Sara was asking was possible, that Christmas didn't have to be over.

"I can't wait for Christmas to come again," she said. "I wish it were tomorrow."

"I wish it were too," I said. "But it's three hundred and sixty-four days until Christmas comes again."

"Too many days," Sara whimpered. "I can't wait that long."

My eyes were still fixed on the bright evening star when a distinct understanding came into my heart. Christmas did not have to be over. It never has to be over. The answer was obvious to me now, and a way to share that answer with my daughter came clearly to my mind.

"Let me tell you a story," I said. "It's a story about a Christmas Day long ago when Grandpa Great was a little boy."

"Grandpa Great who is almost ready to die?" Sara asked.

"Yes. Grandpa Great who lives in the care center and can't get out of bed."

Sara tilted her head back and looked up at me in wonderment. "Grandpa Great was a little boy?" she asked.

"Of course he was," I said. "And he looked forward to Christmas just as much as you do. And he didn't want Christmas to end any more than you do either. And one Christmas he learned how to be as happy on every day of the year as he was on Christmas morning."

"Tell me the story, Daddy," Sara said.

And I did . . .

Jesse lived on a farm a mile from town in a high mountain valley. It was many years ago, before there were buses to carry little boys and girls to school or tractors to plow the fields. In the spring and summertime Jesse helped his father with farm chores. He would heft the heavy harnesses off their hooks in the tack shed and carry them out to the barnyard where his father would drape them over the shoulders and backs of old Buck and Dan, the workhorse team that pulled the plow in spring and the mower and hay wagon in summer. During those long, sun-drenched days that started before daylight and ended well after dusk, Jesse drove the team and wagon through the fields as his father and two hired men pitched hay onto the wagon bed. Then they would ride the wagon to the barn, and Jesse would help pitch hay into the loft until his arms were so tired he thought they might fall off. Day after day, week after week, they would store up the hay for winter.

"We've got to make hay while the sun shines," Jesse's father would say if Jesse looked the least bit like he might complain. "Fall will be here before we know it, and then the snow will fly."

Jesse both dreaded and anticipated the arrival of fall. He dreaded it because it meant he had to go back to school, which meant—rain, snow, or shine—he had to walk the long mile to the little gray schoolhouse in town and then back again each day. Yet in another part of his heart he joyously anticipated fall's arrival because he knew that once the potatoes were in and the harvest was finished, his father would take the old .30-30 rifle down from its rack above the fireplace and they would pull their chairs up to the kitchen table on a golden autumn evening and clean the gun and start to talk about where the big bucks would be running this year.

For Jesse there were two mornings in the year that stood out gloriously from all the rest. One was the morning when he and his father would roll out of their warm beds and set off into the cold darkness in search of their winter supply of venison. The other was Christmas, when Jesse hoped, year after year, to get a rifle of his own.

Jesse often dreamed of the hunt, imagining how it would be that year. Then, when it would finally come, on a magical October morning long before daylight, he would follow his father out through the moon-glazed snow. He would be bundled in his sheepskin-and-denim coat and his cap with the flaps that pulled down over his ears. The icy snow would crunch beneath his boots, and every few steps a boot would break through the crisp top layer of snow as if through a pane of glass. Jesse's leg would sink to the knee, and he would lurch forward against the painfully sharp edge of the snow. Then he would awkwardly pull himself free again and eagerly press forward, undaunted.

By daylight Jesse and his father would be perched on a granite pinnacle above a deep draw in the mountains east of the farm. There they would sit in the silence of the bone-cold morning, looking down into the draw and gazing out across the beautiful valley where the farm lay under a rolling blanket of snow. Before long the deer would begin to move. And finally, after what seemed an eternity, a majestic buck—one that looked suitable to feed the family all winter—would appear out of an oak thicket. Jesse would watch in awe as his father raised the rifle to his shoulder and, with one perfect shot, secured his family's meat supply for the long, hard winter to come.

Jesse admired his father with all his heart. More than anything, he wanted to be just like him. And that is why, more than anything, Jesse wanted a .30-30 rifle of his own that Christmas. He had begun asking for a rifle when he was seven years old. Every fall between the morning of the deer hunt and the morning of Christmas, Jesse would ask the same question each day. First he would ask his mother. Then he would ask his father. "Can I have a rifle for Christmas this year?"

Each time he asked the question, he got one of two answers. "I don't think you're quite old enough yet," or, "We'll see."

Then Christmas morning would come, and Jesse would jump out of his comfortable covers and bundle into his stiff clothes. With the milk bucket in one hand and the coal-oil lantern in the other, he'd make his way out through the icy darkness to the barn where it was his responsibility to milk the cow and feed old Buck and Dan and the broodmares before coming back in to Christmas. In the meantime his father would be down at the stock pens feeding the other cows.

When the chores were all done, the family would meet at the foot of the Christmas tree in the parlor, and Jesse would begin to rustle through the presents Santa had miraculously left the night before. Each year he would pull all the beautifully wrapped packages out from under the tree, praying that somewhere in the pile he would come upon a long, narrow package. And each year his high hopes would eventually dwindle to sharp disappointment as he opened the last of the presents.

Then came the summer when Jesse turned twelve. He was getting bigger every day, and every day he was able to do more to help his father. He took pride in not only driving the team and wagon during hay loading, but in jumping off and helping load the wagon as they made their way down through the forever fields. Jesse's father seemed pleased with his son, and at least once a day he would praise the boy for his good work.

Jesse knew things were truly beginning to change the morning his father put his hand on Jesse's shoulder and told him he had something very important to talk to him about. As they lay in the shade under the hay wagon after eating their lunch that day, his father propped himself up on his elbow and looked at Jesse thoughtfully, the way he looked at a man when he was talking business with him.

"I'm very pleased with the way you help me," his father said. "You're working hard enough now that I should be paying you. I wish I could pay you with money, but we don't have much cash, and what we do have must be saved for necessities. So I want to offer you something else. The new broodmare is going to have a colt this winter. When the colt is born, it will be yours."

Jesse's heart swelled like a balloon, and he sat up with such excitement that his head bumped the bottom of the hay wagon. He rubbed his head and started laughing, and his father began to laugh as well. "You mean the colt will be my own?" Jesse asked when he finally stopped laughing. "My very own?"

"Your very own," his father assured him.

"Could I break him myself and ride him to school?" He had never felt quite so excited, so absolutely grateful.

"Yes," his father said. "He will be yours to do with as you wish, as long as you take care of him properly."

"I'll take care of him better than any horse has ever been cared for," Jesse promised. "You'll see, Dad. I'll break him right and I'll comb his mane and tail every day and I'll see that his feet are kept trim and I'll feed him every morning and night and I'll never run him back to the barn—" Jesse paused to take a breath. "You'll see, Dad. You'll see."

"I know you will, son. And the broodmare will need special care this fall and winter," his father replied. "I didn't know she was with foal when I made the deal with the old horse trader from the desert last spring. The good news is that she's going to have a colt. The bad news is that the colt will be born in the dead of winter, which is a difficult thing up here in the cold mountain country."

"I'll take care of the mare, Dad," Jesse said. "I'll take the best care of her, and everything will be fine no matter how cold it gets this winter."

The rest of the summer passed in a blaze of glory. Every night Jesse lay in bed looking at the dark ceiling of his room, lost in a jumble of thought. He imagined a beautiful blaze-faced colt jumping and prancing out across the meadow. He could see himself next summer, breaking the colt to halter, and the summer after that saddling it for the first time, and then in the fall, climbing up into the saddle and riding his own horse to school. Imagine that—no more walking the long mile to town, but every day riding proudly into the school yard on a long-legged, wonderful horse.

Before he knew it, the soft summer days had stiffened into the crisp days of autumn. Every morning before school Jesse hustled out to the barn to milk the cow and feed old Buck and Dan and the broodmare. The mare was getting larger and larger, and every morning Jesse would drop down onto his chest and roll under the bottom board of the stall. Then he'd stand next to the mare and rub her sleek neck and talk to her at length about the colt inside her and how much he was looking forward to it being born. The mare would turn her head and look at him through her satiny black eyes and nuzzle her face into the warmth of his jacket. Then Jesse would hurry back to the house for breakfast.

On a golden autumn evening that October, Jesse's father hefted the .30-30 rifle down from above the fireplace and laid it on the kitchen table. The two of them sat down and Jesse watched as his father cleaned the gun in preparation for the deer hunt the next morning. His father whistled and his eyes were bright. Jesse thought he had never seen his father this happy before. It had been a good season; the hay loft was full and the potato yield had been better than ever and prices were strong. The excitement of the moment lasted clear through the evening, and Jesse couldn't wait to greet the dawn.

The next morning before daylight, Jesse and his father climbed to the top of a rocky ledge that overlooked a promising draw where deer might well appear as soon as day broke. As they waited in the cold morning quiet, Jesse asked his father if he could look through the rifle's sights, and his father willingly handed him the gun. Jesse brought the butt of the rifle to his shoulder and hoisted the heavy barrel into position. He was pleased at how comfortably the rifle fit him. He was no longer too small for the gun, and his father seemed to notice.

"Won't be long and you'll be the one who bags our winter meat," his father said. Jesse took this as the perfect opportunity to ask the question that hung on the edge of his tongue.

"Do you think I could get a rifle for Christmas this year?" Jesse asked with even more expectation than usual.

"Maybe so," his father said.

Jesse could not believe what he'd heard. It was not, "We'll see," or, "You're not quite big enough yet." It was, *"Maybe so."* The words filled Jesse's heart with wonder and hope, and he looked at his father excitedly, his eyes wide.

"Maybe so," his father repeated with a smile as he clapped Jesse on the back.

Now it was almost impossible to wait for Christmas. Jesse considered himself the luckiest boy in all the world. On feet light as clouds he floated the mile to school each day. After school, he floated all the way home. The thought of having his very own rifle began to upstage every other thought in his mind. Though he continued to check the broodmare and place fresh straw in her stall each morning, and though the last thing he did before going to bed at night was to check her again, he grew less and less concerned for the mare and more and more enthralled with the idea of getting his own rifle. Almost every night he dreamed of beautiful blue-barreled rifles, and he constantly prayed for the days to pass more quickly.

* * *

Finally it was Christmas Eve. The day passed as slowly as a melting icicle, and Jesse spent most of it tromping through the low hills east of the farm, imagining himself with his own gun. He paid little mind to the mare that day. He had grown weary of waiting for the colt to come, and his thoughts glowed with the vision of a brand-new rifle. As the day drew to a close, Jesse knelt in prayer with his mother and father, but his heart pounded so hard and his head was so full of anticipation that he did not hear the words his father prayed.

"Help us remember Him before whom a few gifts were laid in that lowly manger," Jesse's father prayed. "Help us to remember the many gifts He has spread before us, thereby providing an unending Christmas."

As Jesse was caught up in visions of stalking regal bucks with his handsome new rifle, his father continued to pray for the true spirit of Christmas—for the gift of being able to think of others more than self, for the blessing of being able to find joy in giving, and for the ability to understand and appreciate the most important gift of Christmas.

The sound of the words entered Jesse's ears, but their meaning did not register in his heart. He was too full of exhilaration and too swollen with expectation to allow the words of his father's prayer to settle into his soul.

He went to bed that night with his heart galloping in his chest and his mind racing with thoughts of hunting. Not long after Jesse had gone to bed, his father came into the room and sat down on the bed beside him. Jesse saw his father's form as a dark silhouette against the pallid moonlight sifting in from the window.

"Jesse?" his father said as he laid his heavy hand on Jesse's shoulder. "The mare looks awfully close to foaling. Be sure to check her and change her straw first thing in the morning before you come in for Christmas."

"I will," Jesse said.

His father patted him on the shoulder then walked out of the room while Jesse lay there thinking. The mare had seemed ready to foal for days, and every morning for the past week he had plodded out to the barn to check her. Every morning it was the same—the mare standing in the corner of the stall and no colt. Jesse had grown impatient with the morning routine that began with excitement and hope but ended with disappointment. He was pleased that on this night, at least, he could look forward to something else in the morning—and with all his heart he hoped it would be a brand-new .30-30 rifle.

On Christmas morning Jesse awoke as he always did in the cold, early darkness. As he rolled out of the warm covers, he heard the back door softly shut, and he knew his father was already on his way down to the stock pens to feed. Jesse hurried now, realizing he would have to work quickly to finish his chores and get back to the house by the time his father did. He wanted to start opening presents as soon as possible, and the only thing standing between him and the presents were the chores to be done in the barn.

He pulled on his frigid pants, shirt, socks, and boots, then bundled into his coat and put on his cap, pulling the flaps down over his ears. In the kitchen he grabbed his deerskin gloves and lit the coal-oil lamp. With the lamp in his right hand and the milk bucket in his left, out the door into the frosty morning he went. He trotted down the icy path to the barn, catching his balance now and then as his feet slid this way and that. He unlatched the big barn door and slowly pulled it open. The door moaned and groaned in protest of its frozen hinges.

Just inside the door stood the milk cow in her milking stanchion, waiting to be fed her hay and offer up her milk. Jesse hung the lantern on a hook by the door and scurried down to the far end of the barn to the horse stalls. Old Buck's stall was first, then Dan's, then the broodmare's. With the lantern at the other end of the barn, the light was gray and dim.

Jesse went straight to the broodmare's stall and peered skeptically through the boards. He could see the dark shape of the mare; she was standing in the corner like she always did in the morning, and he immediately noted, as he had already mostly expected, that she was standing alone. He didn't give it another thought. There were other things on his mind this morning. His heart leapt as he imagined the rifle in his hands, the heft of its ample weight, the crack of its shot, and the feel of its kick against his shoulder. The mare would have her colt when she would have it. Today was the day for the rifle.

Quickly and with an air of impatience, Jesse tossed a pitchfork full of hay beneath the bottom board of the mare's stall. He was in too big a hurry to change the straw; it was something he could do later. He fed Old Buck and Dan, then hustled back to the other end of the barn and began to milk the cow. His palms and fingers worked in perfect rhythm, and the musty, cold barn filled with the rapid spish-spish-spish of his milking. Never had he filled the bucket so swiftly. He set the lantern and the full, steaming bucket of milk in the snow just outside the barn door. Then he began to push the groaning door closed. As he did so, he thought he heard a sound from the far end of the barn. It was a strange sound, and he stopped silent for a moment and listened carefully in the crisp, still air. There was no more sound until he started to close the door again, and in his haste to get up to the house and open his presents he convinced himself that all he had heard was the moaning of the heavy barn door.

A ribbon of steam trailed from Jesse's mouth as he huffed up the icy path to the house. The promise of Christmas Day was beginning to present itself with a faint hint of light over the mountains to the east. At the house his mother had a cup of steaming cocoa waiting. He sipped it carefully, warming inside as his heart boomed harder and harder in anticipation of discovering what lay beneath the tree in the parlor. His father returned from the stock pens and asked Jesse how the mare was. "Same as every morning," Jesse answered.

Without further delay they went in and started opening presents. Jesse opened a large package and pulled out a splendid, blue denim coat. The coat, lined with sheepskin, was just like his old one, but bigger and new. From another package he pulled a pair of glorious-smelling leather boots, and from another, a bright new pocketknife.

One by one the presents disappeared from beneath the tree until the hard truth finally settled on Jesse. There was not a package remaining under the tree—even with the greatest leap of faith or imagination—that could possibly contain a rifle inside.

Jesse stood up and walked slump-shouldered across the room and sat down heavily on a pinewood chair. He buried his face in his arms, and his mother and father came over and knelt at either side of him.

"You're not quite old enough for a rifle yet," his mother said in a soft, consoling voice.

"The day will come when you will have your rifle," his father promised.

There was a long pause before Jesse finally raised his head. His eyes were moist, and his face was creased with sadness. "I wanted a rifle more than anything," he said sorrowfully.

"I know you did, son," his father said regretfully. "But this was not the year for you to get a rifle. Someday you'll understand."

"It's not fair," Jesse said. "Why couldn't I get it this Christmas? You said I might be able to get it this year. It's too long to wait another year."

"You've received such wonderful gifts this Christmas," Jesse's mother said. "Just look at what you've been given."

Jesse raised his glistening eyes and took stock of all the gifts and bright wrapping strung about the room. But he could not see what his mother saw. He could only see what wasn't there, and he buried his face in his shirtsleeve and sobbed uncontrollably.

The rest of the day Jesse thought of nothing but his misfortune. He bundled up in his new clothes, tucked his new pocketknife into his pocket, and with his shoulders hunched against the bitter wind he set out toward the mountains to the east.

For hours he slogged through the heavy snow, weaving in and out of the tall pines. By midday he found himself sitting on a tower of rock overlooking a magnificent ravine where he imagined the sight of a grand buck prancing down through the glittering trees. But there were no deer in the draws now. They had all moved to lower country. Jesse sat there in the brittle air feeling sorry for himself, thinking of nothing except how unfair it was that he hadn't gotten a rifle for Christmas. His heart was so full of disappointment there was no room for anything else but gloom.

It was late afternoon before he got back to the house. He stomped the snow off his boots on the back porch and stepped through the door into the warm kitchen. The house was full of the smell of turkey and pies, and his mother immediately encircled him in her arms, wondering where he had been and if he was all right. She scolded him for not telling her where he was going or how long he would be gone.

"Where's Dad?" Jesse asked after apologizing.

"He went down to the barn just now," his mother answered.

A horrible dark feeling seized Jesse's heart. Since he had shut the barn door that morning, he had not once thought of the mare. He had been so swallowed up in self-pity he had completely forgotten his responsibility.

Out the door he flew, and down the path he scampered to the barn. He unlatched the heavy door, and with all his might he tugged it open. Soft evening light washed into the barn. Jesse stood in the doorway and peered all the way down to the horse stalls. What he saw in that moment was something he would never forget—not in this life or through all eternity. He saw it with his eyes and at the same time saw it with his heart, and it left him frozen, confounded, and afraid in the bitter-cold doorway of the barn.

Just outside the mare's stall, in a pitiful little heap, lay a motionless newborn colt. Next to the colt knelt Jesse's father.

Jesse started to move but his legs were numb with shock, and he fell in a lump on the icy ground. He gathered himself up, hurried down to the stall, and fell to his knees at the side of a delicate red colt with a beautiful white star on its forehead. Its eyes were closed and it lay perfectly still in the gray light of the barn. Jesse's heart fell like a rock to the bottom of his stomach. He ran his fingers through the colt's soft coat, and he started to cry. He bent over the colt and cried harder and harder and stroked it more and more until, in a moment of simple promise, he felt a hint of warmth pass into his fingers, and he saw the colt's little belly slowly lift and fall in the faintest motion of breathing.

"Is he alive?" Jesse asked.

"Barely," his father said.

"Why is he outside the stall?"

Jesse's father pointed to the space between the bottom board of the stall and the straw-covered ground. It was the space Jesse liked to roll through, rather than open the gate, when entering the stall. It was also the space he tossed the mare's hay through when he fed her every morning and evening. Looking through the gap now, Jesse could see the mare's front knees and hooves prancing nervously on the other side of the fence. He looked up and saw the mare's face hovering over the top board of the stall, her terror-filled eyes glaring down on him. Then he suddenly realized what had happened.

When the mare had lain down to give birth to the colt, she must have settled next to the edge of the stall, and the colt had come into this world beneath the bottom board of the fence—coldly and cruelly separated from its mother. In the same instant he realized what had happened, he comprehended his guilt. The mare in the stall, the colt outside the stall, and both incapable of doing anything about it. Jesse was overcome with shame and remorse. There lay a helpless colt, *his* colt, separated from its mother and in need of warmth and milk, and it was Jesse's fault for not being there when he should have been.

"How long has he been here?" Jesse asked.

"I don't know," his father said. "Judging by how weak he is, and how dry his coat is, and how much tromping the mare has done in her stall, I would say he was probably born about the time we were opening our presents this morning."

Jesse ran his fingers down the colt's neck and admitted to himself how dry its coat was. His father was right. The colt had been in the world long enough for the moisture of its birth to have thoroughly dried. Jesse's heart sank further as he was forced to admit that the colt had probably been born early that morning while he was opening his presents in the house, and that it had lain there through all of Christmas Day, through all the hours that Jesse had sulked about in the mountains. The handsome little red colt had lain there in the frigid air all day. It was a miracle the colt was still alive and hadn't starved.

Still alive! Jesse's thoughts began churning.

"What can we do?" Jesse cried. "We can save him, can't we?"

"I'm afraid it might be too late," his father said. "He's too weak to stand and nurse, and I don't know if the mare will even accept him now."

Jesse instinctively jumped to his feet. Without another thought he ran to the house, a white billow of steam trailing him. From the pantry shelf he grabbed the clear glass bottle and rubber nipple he had used to feed an orphaned calf the previous spring. As he trotted back down the frozen path to the barn, Jesse's eyes rose to the horizon above the mountains, and he saw the first star of the evening. It was a fleeting glance, but the image of the star burned a deep imprint on his heart. When he got back to the barn his father had already haltered the mare and led her out of the stall. The mare stammered around her newborn colt, sniffing and nuzzling it. Strangely enough, she now seemed only mildly interested in the colt, as if it didn't belong to her.

Without even asking his father for advice, Jesse began to stroke the mare and talk to her softly. He worked his way slowly and carefully to her milk sack and prayed that she would allow him to fill the bottle with her warm, life-giving milk. It took several tries and more patience than Jesse had ever mustered, but finally the mare relented and stood still long enough for him to squirt the bottle full of her milk.

He then sat down in the straw and lifted the colt's dainty head onto his lap. He teased the colt's mouth with the nipple for a long, long time before it finally opened its eyes and began to lick at the bead of milk with its dry tongue. Eventually, with some coaching from his father, Jesse finally coaxed the colt to take the nipple into its mouth, and once the starving baby horse began to suck, the bottle quickly emptied.

Jesse repeated the process two more times, milking the mare and nursing the colt. Then his father told him it was enough. The two of them lifted the colt and carried it through the gate into the stall and laid it down on the soiled and grungy straw that Jesse hadn't bothered to change that morning. They led the mare back into the stall and shut the gate. Then Jesse's father said, "We need to leave them alone now."

* * *

Later that night they came back and found the colt still lying in the same place and in the same position where they had placed him earlier. "We'll have to stay with him," Jesse's father said. "We'll have to hand-feed him every half hour or so until he's strong enough to get up and feed himself."

"I'll stay with him," Jesse said. "I'll bring my bedroll out and take care of him until morning."

And that is what Jesse did.

While the rest of the world went to bed, languidly leaving one Christmas Day behind and longingly dreaming of another three hundred sixty-four days away, Jesse stayed up all night with his newborn colt and did everything in his power to keep the slight and frail animal alive until morning. Every thirty minutes he milked the mare and nursed the colt. Between feedings he fell onto his bedroll next to the colt and rested and prayed. He prayed that the colt would live, and he pleaded for forgiveness for neglecting his duties and promised his Heavenly Father he would never be selfish again. As the night passed into early morning, Jesse curled up close to the colt and rubbed its neck and back. He talked to the colt in a soft whisper and told it he was sorry for the way he had acted. "You're the best Christmas gift I could have ever asked for," Jesse said. "Please don't die."

By the light of the coal-oil lamp, Jesse looked into the colt's wondrously dark eyes, and his heart burned with love. He noticed again the beautiful white star on the colt's forehead, and he remembered the lone star over the mountains he had seen the evening before. "If you live," Jesse whispered to the colt, "I will call you Star. And I promise I will take care of you better than any colt has ever been taken care of. I will never forget you again."

As the light of a new day began to filter into the barn, the gangly little horse started fumbling to his feet. Before long he was standing crooked and wobbly on delicate legs, and soon thereafter was feeding himself at his mother's side.

Jesse watched it all with a grateful heart and thanked his Heavenly Father for what he had learned that night. During the long night there had been plenty of time for Jesse to contemplate the gifts that made Christmas so exciting, the fleeting gifts that came and went just as Christmas Day itself did. He thought of gifts anxiously anticipated that only ended up hanging on a wall or sitting on a shelf. But he thought even more about the gifts that were his every day—of parents who loved him, legs to walk on and food to eat, the beautiful mountain valley where he lived, and the warm and comfortable home where he was sheltered every day. And he thought about the gift that started Christmas two thousand years ago—the gift that was signaled by the bright star over Bethlehem. The gift of God's son. These gifts, he came to understand that night, were the most precious of all, and they were gifts that were his every day.

Never again did Jesse allow Christmas to swallow him up in selfish concerns. On that long-ago night after Christmas, he came to understand that the most important gifts were the ones given from the heart, the ones given without thought of self.

And as he grew older, Jesse taught his own family that if they would forget about receiving and concern themselves only with giving, Christmas would never be a disappointment; Christmas would never be over . . .

Sara lay motionless in my lap. There was silence for a very long time. Finally she looked up at me, and my heart warmed as I noticed the light that had returned to her eyes.

"When Star got big, did Grandpa Great ride him to school every day?" Sara asked.

"He certainly did," I said. "And when Grandpa Great turned fourteen, he finally got a beautiful new rifle for Christmas. But that rifle was never so precious to him as his horse named Star. Jesse rode the horse everywhere he went, and every time he looked at that big bright star on his horse's forehead, he thought of what he learned on the night after Christmas when he was twelve years old. And at night when he looked up at the stars in the heavens, he thought of them all as Christmas stars, and he remembered that as long as he cared more about others than about himself, every day of the year could be Christmas."

Sara smiled at me and wrapped her arms around my neck. I looked again out the upper window of the living room and saw that the first star of evening had been joined by a myriad of others. I held Sara tight and whispered in her ear, "Do you still wish Christmas Day wouldn't end?"

She released her hold on me, tilted her head back, and looked at me with all the sincerity of her heart. "No," she said.

"Then what do you wish?" I asked.

"I wish we could go visit Grandpa Great."

And we did.

ABOUT THE AUTHOR

Lyman Hafen has been writing for regional and national audiences for more than twenty years. Born in St. George, Utah, he is a fifth-generation southern Utahn whose Mormon-convert Swiss ancestors settled the village of Santa Clara in the 1860s. His writing, both fiction and nonfiction, has been recognized on seven occasions by awards from the Utah Arts Council. In 1983 he cofounded *St. George Magazine* and was its editor for sixteen years.

Currently he serves as executive director of the Zion Natural History Association in Zion National Park. He has written eight books, including the novel for young readers, *Over the Joshua Slope;* a memoir, *Roping the Wind;* and a biography of Bruce Hurst, *Flood Street to Fenway.* His tale of hope, *In the Midst of Winter,* was hailed by Richard Cracroft as "a gem of a novel."

Practically growing up on horseback, he became a rodeo competitor in high school and college, winning the Utah State High School Rodeo All-Around Championship in 1973, and riding for BYU's rodeo team after his LDS mission to Argentina (1974–76). He retired from riding and began writing as a senior at BYU, and he has never stopped.

He was recently released as bishop of his Santa Clara ward, a calling his great-great grandfather held for twenty-eight years. Today he teaches his son Josh's CTR-6 Primary class. He and his wife Debbie have six children ranging in age from six to twenty-four.